ABOUT THE AUTHOR:

Debra Reyes-
 is a Los Angeles–born writer whose work blends myth, history, and the unseen architecture of the world around us. *Aradia Rising: The Red War* is the third book in her trilogy, completing the opening arc of a saga that spans realms, centuries, and bloodlines.

If you've reached this point in the journey, then you've walked beside her through every vision, every battle, every awakening — and she thanks you for staying.

TABLE OF CONTENTS

Chapter One — The War Machine
Chapter Two — The Signal Beneath the Ruins
Chapter Three — The Gate of Worlds
Chapter Four — The Contract Remembered
Chapter Five — Union and Exile
Chapter Six — The Son of Mars
Chapter Seven — Seraph Nine
Chapter Eight — The Veiled
Chapter Nine — The Red Sky Breaks
Chapter Ten — The Descent of Michael
Chapter Eleven — The Collapse
Chapter Twelve — The Last Light of Mars
Chapter Thirteen — The New Dawn

Epilogue — The Realmwalker

Prologue Voiceover — "The Diseased Century

We called it the zombie age,

waiting for the bodies to rise,

never realizing they already had.

We walked through cities of sleepwalkers, mouths

moving to the rhythm of screens, eyes dimmed by

hunger that no longer belonged to the body.

The infection wasn't blood—it was obedience.

The bite was belief.

And by the time we noticed,

the world had already eaten itself.

War was never an invention; it was a habit. From the first fire to the last flag, humankind kept feeding the same machine—faith against faith, color against color, profit against soul. The empires called it order. We called it infection.

America was the final fever. A nation built on bones and paper promises, preaching liberty while poisoning its own roots. Its leaders rotted from the inside, puppets dangling from strings that reached beyond the stars. The masters were never human—not entirely. They wore flesh when it suited them, power when it didn't. They whispered through markets and satellites, harvesting belief like fuel.

They came first for the keepers of memory—the Indigenous nations, the tribes that remembered the songs of the sky. They burned the drums, silenced the languages, and buried the women who still spoke to thunder. But the land kept our names. And when the empire fell, we were still here—smoke-scarred, but breathing.

Now the same shadows have fled to Mars. The exiles of their own collapse. They burrow beneath the red dust, building a new dominion in the dark. Down there, the native people of Mars—those who hid from the first colonists, those who learned to live in the heat and silence—feel the tremor of ships settling above them.

The disease has found another host, but so has the cure..

Chapter 1 —

The War Machine

MARS — THARSIS ARMORY BELT — NIGHT

Beneath the red dust, the world hums like a buried heart. The surface is a lie of domes and gleaming towers, a stage built for Earth's surviving broadcasts. The true Mars lives below — a hive of heat and iron, tunnels carved through basalt and bone. Entire cities spiral downward: barracks stacked like tombs, furnaces that never cool, rivers of coolant glowing blue in the dark. Down here the air tastes of rust and prayer, and every breath belongs to Helix.

The indigenous of Mars — the ones who hid when the first settlers came — have been dragged into the light again. Their songs are forbidden, their symbols erased, their children turned into engineers of their own captivity. Above them, the escaped elites from Earth sit in glass citadels, ruling a planet they will never touch. They call it salvation, a second Eden. But the ground knows better. It remembers the boot.

It remembers the scream. And somewhere in the labyrinth, the machine's pulse skips — as if the planet itself has begun to dream of rebellion.

Mars breathes like an engine.
 Domes glare against the dark like lacquered eyes; between them, manufactories seethe—rail spines, crucible towers, plating yards, all exhaling a steady, iron heat. Gantries step across the horizon like metal herons. The sky is a red bruise stitched with satellites.

Inside the domes: order.
Outside: obedience.

DUST-BORN file in gray respirators, backs salted with rust. VAT-BORN move like a single organism—precision-grown, eyes bright, wrists lit with ownership sigils. INDENTURED carry ammunition crates stamped HELIX // WAR MATERIAL, each step counted by a metronome buried in the floor. Above them drift Watcher Drones, black ovals that listen like priests.

A siren purrs. A banner unfurls: the double spiral of the HELIX.

Somewhere in the distance, an orbital mass-driver coughs—once, twice—the sound of a god clearing its throat.

EARTH — SALT FLATS / SHRINE OF GLASS — NIGHT (REMOTE VIEW)

A circle of glass lies half-buried in salt, rimmed with old copper charms and a line of ash. The wind sings a dry song. In the circle's warped reflection, Aradia kneels—eyes closed, palms down, the moon caught like a white seed in her dark hair.

Her voice is a thread tugged through the world.

ARADIA (V.O.)
Breathe in the dust. Hear the gear. Follow the smallest noise.

The glass quivers—then opens.

Mars flows up through it.

Not as sight, not as sound. As pressure. As frequency.

She falls—still kneeling, not moving at all—into the red machine.

HELIX CITADEL — GLASS WALK / COMMAND SPINE — NIGHT

(REMOTE VIEW)

The vision rides along a spine of black glass suspended over a cathedral of servers. Red light pulses beneath, timed to the planet's grids. On the far side of the chamber, ten figures stride in formation, boots hushing the floor.

Their speech reaches Aradia in fragments, as if the air itself edits them.

ARCHON KESTREL (fragment, distant)
...output stable... discipline indices hold...

GENERAL STONE (fragment)
...Belt Offensive... window opens in seven—no, six orbits...

DIRECTOR VAR (fragment)
...anomaly persists... opposition phase... same human frequency...

The vision skims past them like a shadow refuses a candle. Aradia does not stay for their words. She follows a pulse. Something *alive*.

MARS — PARADE SQUARE / DAWN SHIFT — NIGHT - DAWN

Searchlights carve lanes through red fog. Rows of Dustborn stand rigid in grit up to their shins. The speaker pylons crackle with catechism:

P.A. VOICE (EVERYWHERE)

Labor is absolution.
Obedience is the atmosphere.
You are the lungs of Mars.

A hush slips across the ranks.

From the barracks gate, HE walks out.

Young. Twenty by Earth's slow clock, not a day more. The uniform sits on him like it decided to be worn: matte black, collar sealed; no bars, no braid—just a thin white sigil at the throat that the drones recoil from and salute at once.

He moves like gravity prefers him.

His eyes are winter glass—clear, assessing, withholding—and when he turns his head the Watcher Drones tilt in unison, as if waiting for the thought to become instruction.

ARADIA (V.O.)

Who taught you to stand with your shoulders like that?

The vision tightens. The world narrows to the tremor of a hand at his side—then calms. He breathes once, and the square breathes with him.

P.A. VOICE
Formation Delta. Brace for inspection. Praise the Helix. Praise the—

He raises two fingers.

Silence drops over the square like a sheet.

He studies the first line—no anger, no warmth, only calculation—then stops before a Dustborn boy whose respirator is too large for his face.

The young commander's gaze flickers—one beat—at the boy's clenched fist. A chalk smear. A small symbol there, rubbed fast: an eye inside a crescent, a thin line of fire.

Aradia's pulse stumbles.

ARADIA (V.O.)
Mine.

He says nothing. The boy lowers his hand. The commander moves on.

The Watcher Drone nearest the symbol glitches—a single static click—then smooths.

HELIX TRAINING HALL — EDGE OF THARSIS — NIGHT (REMOTE VIEW)

Steel. Glass. Breath freezing white. Targets lift out of the floor and track across air like silver birds.

The young commander stands at the line. A rifle rests along his forearm—the stock modified, the weight wrong, the balance perfect. No stance anyone taught him exactly; a stance remembered by the body.

He waits.

Targets bloom, accelerate, split.

He fires.

Air stitches itself shut behind the rounds. Every impact is silent and precise—center, center, center—until a decoy flares and he doesn't fire, and the range lights blink an approving blue.

A technician leans in, offers a new magazine. He shakes his head.

He closes his eyes.

When he opens them again, the targets are already dying.

Aradia feels the decision before the shots. It's her own rhythm—mirrored, inverted, sharpened to a blade.

Her breath fogs the glass circle on Earth.

ARADIA (V.O.)
Who taught you, me?

He unloads the rifle, sets it down, palms skimming metal like a farewell. The techs pretend not to stare. One makes the sign of the double spiral; another, the sign of the old cross—small, ashamed.

The commander looks up at a mezzanine window—dark glass, watching. For one second the pane reflects not his face but a smear of starlight and a wing folded like a knife.

Then just glass again.

HELIX CITADEL — LOW CHAMBER / TACTICS NAVE — NIGHT

(REMOTE VIEW)

A table of basalt veined with meteoric nickel. Maps glow in red and bone-white—orbital chains, rail spines, the elevator thread. Voices fall like dice.

Aradia does not catch what they plan; she catches how the room listens. The silence when the young commander enters is not deference. It is expectation.

STONE (fragment, almost proud)
…predictive edge… thirty-one moves ahead in live combat… born for war…

KOH (soft fragment)
…Godfather has reviewed the sequence…

A stillness in the air like a smile without a mouth.

The young commander rests his hands on the stone. He studies the orbits like prayer beads. He tilts his head—fraction, fraction—then moves one glyph.

The plan rearranges itself obediently.

In Aradia's bones a chord she hasn't played in centuries vibrates back.

ARADIA (V.O.)
No. No, not a weapon. Not you.

Her fingertips lift from the glass. They tremble. The vision tries to hold. It slides.

A frequency rises under the chamber's noise—thin, bright, almost beyond hearing—the tone a mother learns in the first hour after a birth.

It cuts straight through her.

The young commander stiffens. He looks up. Not at any person. At the air, at the angle of a circle not present.

For a heartbeat, he looks right at her.

And nothing in him changes.

A tech coughs. The spell breaks. The room breathes again.

MARS — MANUFACTORY CAUSEWAY / SHIFT TURN — NIGHT

Heat shimmers. Conveyor cathedrals drum. A line of Vatborn walks the causeway in perfect five-step cadence, each with a crate balanced at the same angle, sweat rising in the same arc of steam. Their eyes glance—together—to the catwalk overhead.

The young commander passes above, flanked by two officers that the drones refuse to see. A girl below—Indentured, gray scarf, hands raw—looks up through the rail slats and presses a scrap of paper to her mouth.

On it, charcoal-dark, the same small symbol: an eye in a crescent split by a line of fire.

A Watcher centers over her.

Aradia's vision reaches instinctively—soft as breath, hard as lightning—touching the girl's knuckles. The paper warms. The symbol brightens for the time of a single blink.

The drone's lens opens. Then closes. It floats on.

Above, the young commander pauses without turning his head. His throat works once, like someone swallowing a word that doesn't exist in his language.

He keeps walking.

EARTH — SALT FLATS / SHRINE OF GLASS — NIGHT

Aradia tears out of the trance like surf breaking. The wind runs cold hands through her hair. The world is too quiet, too blue, too alive.

She doesn't realize she's on her feet until she's already moving. The sand rasps under her boots. Far out on the flats, lightning sketches a horizon that isn't there.

She presses both palms to the glass. It gives a little, like the top of a sleeping chest.

ARADIA
Who put you there?
(beat)
Who took you from me?

A shadow falls over the circle. David steps into the edge of the moonlight—coat open, eyes like a storm deciding which coast to ruin.

He studies her face. He knows this silence. He's worn it before.

DAVID
What did you see?

She doesn't look at him. She keeps her eyes on the reflection of a boy that the glass does not show.

ARADIA
A machine. Our machine, wearing a stranger's voice.
(a breath)
And a hand I taught before I ever held it.

David's jaw moves, stops. His laugh, when it comes, is a sound with no humor in it.

DAVID
You're shaking.

ARADIA
No.
(then, honest)
Yes.

He follows the line of her hands to the circle. The copper charms clink like small bells. For a moment his reflection and hers overlap with the white seed of the moon, and they look like a single face made of two.

DAVID
Say what you won't say.

Aradia closes her eyes. Inside them: a training hall, silent shots, winter-glass eyes. A symbol in chalk. A target that never should have been missed and never was.

She opens them.

ARADIA
He moves like me.

(beat)

ARADIA (softer)
He looks like you.

The wind goes very far away.

David's mouth shapes a name and does not release it.

Somewhere above the flats, a satellite blinks—on, off—like a nervous star. In the black behind it, something listens.

MARS ORBIT — DAWN

The planet turns like a rust coin under shallow water. The orbital elevator glows faintly as it threads from sky to ground. Around it, a crown of platforms glitters—rail cannons, docks, teeth.

A sensor ping ripples the dark—lonely, exact.

In the citadel below, a bishop-quiet alarm wakes without sound.

The young commander lifts his head in a room where no one is speaking. He listens to something only he can hear.

His pulse slows. Then steadies.

He looks—not up, not down—through.

Aradia, on Earth, sets her hands flat on the glass as if she could hold the world together by touch alone.

The circle hums.

Chapter 2 — Ash and Signal

Earth breathes again, but each breath sounds borrowed. The skies have cleared just enough to remember what blue was, yet the air still tastes of iron and ghosts. The wars are over, the broadcasts gone, but the people move like those still waking from anesthesia — murmuring, rebuilding, forgetting. They call this peace. Aradia knows it is only remission.

In the wastelands once called Arizona, the Remnants have turned an old solar field into a listening post. Towers lean like ribs above the sand; their mirrors no longer catch sunlight but the static of the cosmos. Nightly, they sweep the heavens for proof that humanity did not simply dream itself extinct.

Tonight the wind carries a different hum. A sound layered inside the static: three short bursts, a pause, then a long, rising tone that vibrates the bones. It travels through the antennae, through the copper veins of the desert, through the scar on Aradia's palm — and settles behind her eyes.

We thought the apocalypse would end in fire, she thinks. *But it ended in forgetting.*

The others in the outpost crowd around the receiver. The signal is faint, steady, deliberate. Its pattern matches nothing known to Earth. Old code tables translate fragments:

HELIX // ASCENSION // PHASE II.

Aradia listens deeper. Beneath the mechanical rhythm she hears something else — a heartbeat that isn't the planet's. It feels young. It feels familiar. Every pulse of it repeats the same message in silence: *Come home.*

She steps outside into the cold desert night. Above her, the sky looks healed, but she can taste the old disease still swimming in the air — the obedience, the fear, the half-life of people who once worshiped their chains. The stars blink like open wounds, and somewhere among them glows the faint red eye of Mars.

The signal hums again, clearer this time, as though it recognizes her. Aradia closes her eyes. The desert fades. The machine below Mars stirs. And the distance between them shortens by a single heartbeat.

Earth breathes again, but each breath sounds borrowed. The skies have cleared just enough to remember what blue was, yet the air still tastes of iron and ghosts. The wars are over, the broadcasts gone, but the people move like those still waking from anesthesia — murmuring, rebuilding, forgetting. They call this peace. Aradia knows it is only remission.

In the wastelands once called Arizona, the Remnants have turned an old solar field into a listening post. Towers lean like ribs above the sand; their mirrors no longer catch sunlight but the static of the cosmos. Nightly, they sweep the heavens for proof that humanity did not simply dream itself extinct.

Tonight the wind carries a different hum. A sound layered inside the static: three short bursts, a pause, then a long, rising tone that vibrates the bones. It travels through the antennae, through the copper veins of the desert, through the scar on Aradia's palm — and settles behind her eyes.

We thought the apocalypse would end in fire, she thinks. *But it ended in forgetting.*

The others in the outpost crowd around the receiver. The signal is faint, steady, deliberate. Its pattern matches nothing known to Earth. Old code tables translate fragments:

HELIX // ASCENSION // PHASE II.

Aradia listens deeper. Beneath the mechanical rhythm she hears something else — a heartbeat that isn't the planet's. It feels young. It feels familiar. Every pulse of it repeats the same message in silence: *Come home.*

The sound fades. Silence returns to the desert like a slow tide. For a moment she stands motionless, unsure whether it was real or memory, dream or warning. Then exhaustion folds over her, heavy as sand.

She wakes to dawn. Pale light creeps through the torn canvas of the tent. Outside, the desert glows the color of ash and honey; wind hums against the solar panels like the low note of a cello.

Beside her lies **Loki**—the human shell that still answers to *David*. He's asleep, one arm thrown over his eyes, mouth curved in that half-smile that used to mean trouble and now just means *alive.* For a heartbeat she almost believes in the peace they were promised.

Then the static begins again.

A rusted field radio crackles on the workbench near the door. No one's touched it in months; its batteries should be dead. The voice that slips through it is thin, broken by distance.

"—adia…—dia…signal confirmed…—red orbit…"

Aradia sits up so fast the cot moans. Loki stirs.

"What is it?" he mumbles.

"Listen."

The radio shrieks once, then steadies into the same three-beat pattern she heard last night. Three short bursts, a pause, one long tone. The tent's metal frame begins to tremble in sympathy.

David (Loki) swings his legs over the side of the cot, runs a hand through his hair. "Could be atmospheric interference."

"No," she whispers. "It knows my name."

Outside, the horizon flickers—heat mirage, or something brighter. The sand ripples as though a subterranean drum just struck.

Loki stands beside her now, both of them facing the sound. The radio's light shifts from green to crimson. Words try to form in the static: HELIX…PROJECT…SERAPH— then dissolve into a low, human breath.

Aradia closes her eyes. The echo of the pulse vibrates in her ribs. Somewhere deep in the dark of Mars, a young voice stirs from sleep, hearing her in return.

Distance, she realizes, *has nothing to do with space. Only with memory.*

David looks at her—really looks—and understands that whatever peace Earth offered is about to end.

"We're going back," she says.

The radio hums its agreement. The morning wind tastes of iron again.

Chapter 3 —

Ghosts of the Surface

Purpose in the arc

Transition chapter.

Aradia and Loki leave the fragile peace of Earth behind and enter the liminal space between planets—where signals blur, time folds, and history begins to repeat. On Mars, Helix scientists and guards harvest resources from the domes near the surface. The "indigenous Martians," long forced underground, are starting to re-emerge; their songs cause malfunctions in Helix machinery. The machine fears what it cannot decode.

Emotional tone

Isolation, homesickness, and the weight of déjà vu. A sense that Mars is both new and ancient—its dust carrying the memory of every world that fell before.

Opening scene

Between worlds, there is no sound.
The ship hums without engine or flame, drifting inside the corridor that folds between Earth and Mars. Static crawls along the hull like frost. Aradia watches the red disc growing ahead of them through a window rimmed with prayer etchings. Loki stands beside her, hands deep in his coat pockets, eyes on the same horizon he once called home.

"You feel it too," he says.

"Every breath of it."

Mars is no longer the planet they remember—its thin atmosphere stitched with metallic clouds, its surface buried under mirrored domes that glitter even in darkness. The domes look empty from orbit, but sensors whisper of movement inside.

They break atmosphere in silence. The ship sinks through storms of red dust that spiral like ghosts rising from old graves. Lightning crawls horizontally across the sky, blue against crimson. Below, the uppermost outposts of Helix stretch like scars—parabolic mines, energy siphons, glass cathedrals half-buried in sand.

Aradia feels the psychic field long before they land: a constant murmur of fear, a million minds pressed against stone. The indigenous of Mars still sing, even if only in thought. The sound of their language makes the gauges flutter, the lights dim.

Loki glances at her. "They're still alive."

"For now."

The ship touches down on an abandoned transport pad at the rim of an old crater. Around them, the wind carries the scent of ozone and rust. Out in the haze, shadowed figures move—miners, slaves, or something older. When the gusts thin for a heartbeat, Aradia sees their eyes reflecting gold fire.

One of the figures raises a hand, tracing a spiral in the air. The dust obeys, swirling into the symbol of the *Eye and Crescent*.

Aradia's pulse answers before her voice can. The spiral collapses into nothing, leaving only sand and silence.

Loki's whisper drifts through the comm static. "Ghosts of the surface."

She nods. "No. Survivors."

In the distance, a beacon flares—the same crimson tone that woke her on Earth. It blinks three times, pauses, then once more. The signal is guiding them downward, toward the tunnels where Helix built its empire and where the truth waits buried.

Toward him.

The dead never left.

They just changed coordinates.

Long before rockets, the Earth was mapped by vibration — by ley lines that cut through mountains, deserts, and seas. The old tribes called them songpaths, the Europeans called them dragon veins, and the Church renamed them heresy. But the gates were always there, humming beneath the skin of the world. Some were buried by fear, others by design. A few were never closed at all.

Aradia and David spend weeks following the whispers. Every night, the signal from Mars grows louder — sometimes in dreams, sometimes bleeding through static radios or flickering streetlamps. They travel north through the ruins of Colorado, into lands where the air feels thin and time stutters. The Remnants call this region The Corridor.

One night they find it — a valley where the earth glows faintly blue beneath its own shadow. Old petroglyphs mark the stone walls: spirals, crescents, and something newer —

a carved Helix symbol, burned into the rock as if someone tried to overwrite it.

David kneels and presses his palm to the ground. The soil hums.

"It's open," he says. "But unstable."

"Unstable means alive," Aradia replies.

The wind moves strangely here. It doesn't pass through them, it passes around them. The stars above the valley flicker out of sync — two skies phasing like reflections in shifting water. She feels it then: the same pulse from Mars, now echoing under her ribs. Every heartbeat of the planet calls to its twin.

David looks up. "This isn't a gate built by Helix."

"No," she says. "This one remembers us."

Lightning folds inward instead of down. The air fractures — light without heat, color without form. The valley becomes an hourglass of dust and stars, and at its throat is a doorway made of silence.

Aradia steps forward first. The ground trembles but doesn't resist. David reaches for her hand, fingers brushing the mark on her wrist — the triple moon, glowing faintly in the storm.

"If this is the wrong one?" he asks.

"Then it'll remember where we belong."

The moment they cross the threshold, sound inverts. The earth screams softly, like a newborn remembering air. The valley disappears. The portal swallows them whole.

*For an instant there is nothing—no sky, no ground, only the hum of two worlds aligning.
Then red dust..*

Mars.

And in the dark beneath its crust, something that knows their names.

The first breath burns.

Aradia coughs, tasting iron and ozone. When her vision clears she realizes they aren't standing on a surface at all; they're inside it. A vault stretches above them, walls glinting with veins of quartz and something that looks like obsidian but moves like liquid. The air hums with a low, constant drone, the heartbeat of a world turned inward.

"Underground," David murmurs. His voice sounds smaller here, swallowed by the depth.

Aradia nods. "Exactly where we were meant to be."

Along the tunnel walls she can see carvings—spirals, figures with elongated skulls, hands raised toward stars. Each symbol pulses faintly when her shadow touches it. She traces one with her fingertips and the memory comes unbidden: stories told around desert fires, of the Ant People who lived beneath the earth when the surface burned. They sheltered the first humans, taught them to plant and build, then vanished when the world healed.

"Hopi called them Ant People," she whispers. "Others said they came from the sky. Maybe both were right."

David kneels, brushing dust from a metal brace. "These tunnels aren't ancient. They've been rebuilt. Reinforced."

She looks down the corridor—rails, cables, dim blue lights that fade into infinity. The legends weren't myths; they were maps. The Ant People's cities had become Helix's foundations. Humanity had simply inherited someone else's refuge.

A tremor rolls through the floor. Distant machinery stirs, rhythmic, deliberate. Aradia closes her eyes and listens. The pulse matches the radio pattern from Earth. Each throb carries a whisper of thought, young and fierce and lost.

"He's down there," she says.

David's hand finds hers. "Then we follow the old stories."

The lights flicker in sequence, forming a path into the dark. Carvings glow like embers, guiding them deeper into the veins of Mars—into the place where myth, memory, and bloodline converge.

And somewhere far below, the descendants of the Ant People pause in their labor, lift their heads, and begin to sing.

Chapter 4 — The Contract

The deeper they walk, the quieter the world becomes. Sound thins until only pulse remains—hers, his, the planet's. The lights strung along the tunnel walls flicker in a rhythm that isn't electricity but heartbeat.

Aradia touches the wall again; warmth seeps into her skin and a whisper follows, a thousand voices layered into one: *remember the vow.*

"What vow?" David asks. But she already knows.

The rock splits open like a curtain, revealing a chamber of black glass etched with lines of light. Symbols spiral across the floor, half Theban, half geometry of stars. In the center waits a slab, smooth as water. On it glows a sigil shaped like an eclipse—the mark of Heaven and Hell intertwined.

The Contract.

She steps closer. Every cell in her body hums with recognition. It isn't paper or code; it's living matter, a covenant written into the particles of creation. The air ripples as if aware of her.

A voice rises from the glass, not male or female but both, carrying the weight of two divine lineages.

VOICE
Two halves of one flame. When you loved across the divide, the heavens split. To preserve balance, a vow was sealed: your memories, your child, your dominion, all hidden until the cycle resets.

Images flood her mind—Diana's silver eyes weeping as the seal is cast; Lucifer's hand burning with light as he signs it; David, kneeling, his wings shattering into smoke. The memory is so strong it drops her to her knees.

David catches her, but his own reflection wavers. For a moment his eyes flash that impossible blue—the **Loki** within surfacing.

"We did this," he says, voice breaking. "We swore to forget—to protect him from both realms."

The chamber responds. Columns of light rise, projecting the original glyphs of the pact. Lines connect them like circuitry. The pattern shows three seals still active—one over Earth, one over Mars, one deeper, unnamed. The contract hasn't been broken; it's *counting down.*

"If it expires," Aradia whispers, "the war starts again."

"Unless we rewrite it."

She looks up at him. "Can gods rewrite what they swore before creation?"

He almost smiles. "Only if they remember why they swore it."

The light around them dims. The sigil at the center of the floor shifts, revealing a new symbol—a **circle within a serpent**, ancient and familiar. The mark of the *Ouroboros*.

Aradia reaches out. The moment her fingers brush the light, it fractures into twelve shards that shoot off down separate tunnels. Each shared a key, a witness, or a weapon.

The chamber stills.

"What did you do?" David asks.

"I opened it," she says. "Now every side will know the seals are weakening."

Above them, far beyond the crust, Mars begins to tremble. In the Helix citadel, alarms start to wail. And in the lowest vault, a young man pauses mid-training, his heartbeat syncing to the same pattern as the ancient vow he doesn't yet remember signing.

Michael.

Chapter 5 — Union and Exile

The light from the shattered contract still hangs in the air when the chamber begins to breathe. Dust rises, then falls upward, turning into a spiral of gold. The tunnel walls fade into the sky, the glass floor into a sea of white fire. Time folds until "before" and "after" are the same heartbeat.

Aradia blinks and she is no longer standing in the tunnels of Mars. She is in the beginning.

There is no planet here, no boundary between heaven and void. Only two presences—light and flame—circling one another like cautious stars. When they touch, the universe inhales.

Diana descends first: silver, graceful, her aura a soft lunar tide that cools every storm. Opposite her rises Lucifer, radiant as dawn, carrying the weight of all that burns but does not die. Between them drifts a third light—*the idea of creation itself.*

When they speak, their voices form worlds.

DIANA
"He was never meant to be a weapon."

LUCIFER
"He was meant to be continued balance. Our union is the equation the heavens forbid."

In the haze around them, the first constellations spark. Oceans condense. The seed of Earth is planted. The contract that will one day bind them does not yet exist, but its shadow already stretches across eternity.

Then she feels him—*David*—emerging from the pattern, forged where order meets chaos. The one who walks between realms. She remembers the first moment she saw him: standing at the border of time, eyes full of stormlight, smiling as if he'd already broken every rule to reach her.

ARADIA (V.O.)
I never believed in forbidden things until I became one.

They meet not in body but in resonance. His energy wraps around hers, slow and deliberate, the way dawn wraps a planet. Their joining births color where there was only vibration. Galaxies spill from the pressure of it, stars blooming like embers in their wake.

When the universe can't contain them anymore, they fall—through dimensions, through ages, into flesh. They land in a world still soft with clay and rain. They take names, take breath, build temples that will one day crumble into myths.

But love that bridges light and shadow has gravity, and gravity always calls the gods to account.

The angels come first, cloaked in law, bearing scrolls that glow like blades. Behind them walk the Thrones—empty shells of judgment, blind to mercy. They offer the choice: renounce the union or be exiled beyond the spheres.

Lucifer laughs first. Diana does not. Her tears become comets, streaking across the firmament. The contract is written in that light—two signatures carved into the code of existence, a promise and a punishment intertwined.

We will forget.

We will wander.

We will return when the balance breaks again.

The vision cracks like glass. The white fire fades. Aradia drops back to her knees in the Martian chamber, gasping. David catches her before she falls.

"You saw it too," he says, voice rough.

She nods. "We didn't fall because of pride. We fell because of love."

The air between them trembles—memory overlapping with present, love rewriting itself back into the story.

Somewhere below, deep in Helix's labyrinth, Michael feels a pulse he can't name and looks up toward the surface. For the first time in his life, he feels warmth that isn't fire.

…The angels come first, cloaked in law, bearing scrolls that glow like blades. Behind them walk the Thrones—empty shells of judgment, blind to mercy. They offer the choice: renounce the union or be exiled beyond the spheres.

Lucifer laughs first. Diana does not. Her tears become comets, streaking across the firmament. The decree is carved into the pulse of matter itself—a covenant that tears light from light, scattering what once was whole.

The world fractures.

Glass without edges, stars without names. The explosion of creation becomes a field of shards spinning in every direction—each one a lifetime waiting to be lived. Through them Aradia and David fall, separate yet tethered by the same thread of fire.

Every piece of the universe carries a sliver of their bond.

The shards slow. The pieces drift back together, drawn by a gravity older than law. The brightness compresses, folding space into shape, until she feels his hand again—warm, human, now.

The chamber reforms around them: the black glass floor, the veins of light crawling like nerves. They're kneeling face-to-face, breathing hard. The universe has just closed its wound, and they are the scar that remains.

David meets her eyes. He doesn't need to ask. The knowledge moves between them like current.

A child. Ours. Hidden here.

They rise in unison. The symbols under their feet flare once more, pointing deeper into the labyrinth. The sound that follows isn't thunder but a heartbeat—strong, defiant, waiting.

Aradia grips David's hand. "We will find him," she says.

"We end this," he answers.

And the light obeys, opening a path toward the core of Mars.

The floor beneath them flexes, not with quake but with breath.

The tunnels inhale, exhale—walls swelling, contracting, a heartbeat made of stone and heat. Light ripples through mineral veins in concentric patterns, blooming like mandalas under their feet. Each pulse sends a faint vibration through their bones; every chamber seems to echo the rhythm of a giant heart hidden deeper below.

Aradia steadies herself against the wall. "It's alive."

"Not alive," David says, eyes tracking the rhythm. "Awake."

The corridor bends ahead of them, a serpentine artery lined with bio-metal struts. Vapors coil from vents; red dust rises and falls in sync with the beat. Somewhere in the distance machinery grinds—too regular to be chaos, too mechanical to be natural.

They move fast, boots clanging on iron ribs. The air thickens, warmer, humid with the scent of ozone and iron. Every few steps a glyph flares on the wall, registering their presence. The planet is *recognizing* them, testing its own pulse against theirs.

A sudden surge—then stillness.

From the dark ahead comes a low resonance, a note that hums through the ground, through their chests. David stops. "That's not the planet."

"No," Aradia breathes. "That's him."

The vibration builds into thunder. Lights burst down the corridor like a wave of red fire. Alarms echo far away—Helix sensors tripped by an energy signature they've never recorded before. Drones scramble, mechanical wings slicing the dust.

Aradia draws her weapon from the sheath at her back; David's eyes sharpen, the edge of Loki flickering in their blue sheen. They run.

The hallway opens into a vast, spherical chamber. At its center hangs a mass of rotating rings and light—part engine, part heart. Cables stretch from it like veins, feeding power to every level of Mars. Each rotation sends another wave of the same pulse through the floor.

Aradia feels it in her chest again, stronger, faster. *Michael's heartbeat, amplified.*

"The core's in resonance with him," David says. "They've chained the planet to his pulse."

She looks at the web of cables disappearing into the depths. "Then we follow the arteries."

They dive into the lower conduit, red light strobing around them, alarms echoing down miles of tunnel. The machine above roars to life, awakening the entire Helix network.

Somewhere far below, a young man opens his eyes, the rhythm of the planet drumming in his veins.

Michael.

His gaze turns upward, sensing movement—two signatures, bright as suns, breaking through the network that has kept him captive. For the first time, he doesn't follow the command in his head. He listens to the pulse instead.

The world breathes once more, and the war truly begins.

Chapter 6 — The Stolen Child

The day on Mars begins without sunrise. Light seeps up from the tunnels, silver and blood-red, washing the command citadel in a perpetual dusk. From the balcony of the highest tower, Gabriel watches his army assemble—columns of soldiers in mirrored armor, banners breathing the Helix spiral. The sound of their march is the pulse of a single organism.

Beside him stands Michael—taller than the rest, broad-shouldered, the weight of his heritage hidden behind the insignia of a general. His eyes, pale gold under the armor's glow, scan the ranks with quiet precision. He was raised here, trained here, taught to see order as mercy. To the Helix, he is perfection: a Nephilim bred for obedience and victory.

Gabriel studies him the way a sculptor studies a masterpiece. "You see how they move," he says softly. "Discipline is a kind of grace. Remember that."

Michael nods. "Grace is survival."

"Good." Gabriel's smile is thin, almost human. "Today you lead the outer campaign. The miners in Sector Nine refuse conscription. Bring them back into harmony."

"If they resist?"

"Then remind them what harmony costs."

The general bows his head. "Yes, Father."

The word lands between them like an echo that doesn't fade. Gabriel allows it; he even touches Michael's shoulder, brief, careful, as if the gesture might betray him. For all his rhetoric about order, he loves this boy—the only being in centuries who looks at him without fear.

When Michael leaves, the command room empties into silence. Gabriel turns toward the great window and lets the mask slip for a heartbeat. In the reflection he sees the faint outline of wings that no longer open, and the weight of the lie he's told every day since the boy could speak.

You were born from heaven's fire, he once said. *You are my son.*

The truth—that Michael was taken, not born—has become a wound that even Gabriel fears to touch.

In the field, the war machine moves like a storm. Dropships carve red wakes through the thin atmosphere; dust lifts in spirals around the marching lines. Michael walks at the front, helmet under his arm, the ground trembling beneath each step. The Nephilim in him shows in every motion—effortless power, impossible balance.

To the soldiers he is divine. To himself he is a weapon tempered in Gabriel's voice.

The rebels they confront are miners—gaunt, dust-coated, their tools turned to rifles. When they see him approach, their courage falters. He stops a few meters away and lowers his helmet to his side.

"Lay down your arms," he says, voice calm, resonant. "You will be fed. You will work. You will live."

"We will die free," one of them answers.

Something shifts in him then—an ache, a spark of recognition. Their faces remind him of dreams he doesn't speak of: open skies, voices that call him by a name Gabriel forbids.

He hesitates. Just long enough for the first shot to be fired.

Instinct takes over. He moves faster than thought, deflecting rounds, disarming, subduing—not killing. When the dust settles, the rebels are on their knees, alive. His own troops stare at him, uncertain.

"Take them to the shelters," he orders. "Feed them. The campaign is over."

From orbit, Gabriel watches the feed in silence. The boy's mercy is a crack in perfect obedience. Yet Gabriel cannot bring himself to condemn it. Instead he whispers to the empty air:

"So you did inherit her heart after all."

The feed flickers, static rippling through the image. For an instant the screen shows something that should not be possible—a woman's face, eyes dark with fire, watching the same battle from beneath the planet's crust. Gabriel freezes, hand tightening on the console.

Aradia

He knows now that she is here, and that his borrowed son has begun to feel her pull. Outside, alarms begin to wail, but Gabriel only stands at the window, whispering a prayer no heaven will hear.

"Not yet," he says to the storm. "Please… not yet."

The command tower trembles as the troop carriers return. Through the haze of red dusk, Gabriel watches Michael stride from the landing bay, helmet under one arm, armor scarred with dust but unstained by blood. The boy looks every inch the savior Helix promised its citizens—strong, merciful, terrifying.

Mercy. The word tastes foreign in Gabriel's mouth.

"You spared them," he says when Michael enters the strategy hall.

"They were starving," Michael replies simply. "They believed rebellion was their only voice."

"And so you taught them silence."

"No," Michael says, meeting his gaze. "I taught them hope."

Gabriel turns away before the boy can see his expression. Behind him, the door seals with a sigh.

"Report to debriefing," he orders. "We'll discuss this deviation later."

When Michael is gone, the chamber fills with the smell of ozone and the faint chiming of energy gates opening. **Samael** steps through the light—taller, darker, wings folded like knives. The older archangel carries the cold authority of Heaven itself.

"You are losing him," Samael says without preamble.

"He completed the mission."

"Not the way we designed." Samael circles the table, eyes on the holographic feed of the miners being escorted to shelter. "He hesitated. He *felt*. You should have culled that part of him when you had the chance."

"I tried." Gabriel's voice is low. "Every day. And every day he finds it again."

Samael's stare sharpens. "Then destroy him before he remembers who he is."

Gabriel's hand curls on the console. "He *is* who I made him."

"No," Samael answers. "He is what *she* made possible."

The silence that follows is heavy, dangerous. For a heartbeat Gabriel considers drawing the blade at his hip, but Samael's wings flare—white fire—and the thought dies.

"Do not let sentiment undo us again," the elder archangel says. "The Council is watching. If he falters, both of you burn."

With that, the light folds and Samael is gone. The tower returns to its hum.

Gabriel sinks into the nearest chair. On the table the tactical map still glows, displaying every tunnel and reactor coil that laces the planet. In the center, one line blinks red—deep beneath the crust, a sector newly reactivated.

The old tunnels.

He exhales through his teeth. "You're coming for him, aren't you?"

Beneath those same tunnels, Aradia and David halt mid-step as the ground quivers. A shockwave rolls through the rock, scattering dust in a circular pattern that expands like ripples from a single point far above.

Aradia presses a hand to the wall; warmth floods her palm. A voice, faint but certain, brushes the edge of her mind: *I taught them hope.*

She smiles, eyes bright with the recognition she doesn't try to name. "He's alive."

David looks up toward the ceiling of stone. "And closer than we thought."

In the distance, the heartbeat of Mars quickens—steady, human, defiant. The machine has begun to doubt its own gods.

Chapter 7 — Seraph 9

Core idea

The "new civilization" on Mars is a façade: corporate elites from Earth and their unnamed extraterrestrial patrons built domes and factories on the surface through Helix. The indigenous Martians work as miners and builders under "protective supervision." Michael (Seraph 9) commands the army that keeps the arrangement stable—until he begins to see what the stability costs.

From orbit, the colonies gleam like scattered halos—circles of light pressed into the red dust, radiant and sterile. They call themselves the **Seeletes**, meaning *Those Who See*. Descendants of Earth's surviving aristocracy and the architects of every quiet tyranny before the Fall, they left the dying planet proclaiming that vision itself was purity—that those who could "see beyond the veil" were chosen to inherit the stars..

They do not call what they built a colony. They call it *Continuance*.

The Seeletes made their ascent through a pact written in plasma and deceit, signed not with Heaven or Hell, but with something in between—the silent extraterrestrial brokers once called the *Contractors*. To the Helix, they are known as the *Veiled*. They provided Mars with its atmosphere shields, its power cores, its genetic enhancement tech. In return, they were given rights to the indigenous—those whom the old myths called the Ant People.

The Ant People lived in harmony beneath the crust, their tunnels stretching into miles of crystalline warmth. They were builders, memory-keepers, the first children of Mars before Earth's refugees arrived. Now they labor as slaves under the very domes that suffocate the planet's breath. Their songs—ancient harmonic frequencies—are forbidden, for when they sing, the machines obey them instead of the Seeletes.

And above them all, standing between the Seeletes and the Veiled, commands one man—the General they call **Seraph 9.**

The Helix army drills under an artificial sky. Dome Ares glows with a filtered blue hue that pretends to mimic daylight, but the air is heavy, manufactured, wrong. Michael watches from the command balcony, the cape of his armor brushing the metal railing as ranks of soldiers march with mechanical precision.

To his right, a Seelete delegate named Korrin Vale stands dressed in white. His voice hums with synthetic enhancement—half human, half machine.

"The Contractors have concerns about the miners," Korrin says. "The Ants have begun their chanting again. Harmonic interference. Reactor cores are responding."

Michael doesn't look at him. "They're not ants."

"A figure of speech," Korrin replies, smiling faintly. "You know how language evolves."

"You mean how it erases."

Korrin studies him for a moment. "General, the Seeletes appreciate your compassion, but harmony demands obedience. The tunnels below Sector Nine are off limits. Let Helix handle containment."

"Helix is my command."

"Precisely." The smile widens. "Contain it."

Later, in the observation bay, the hum of the reactors becomes almost melodic. The vibrations rise through the metal floor and into Michael's chest. He closes his eyes, letting the rhythm pulse through him—and then he hears it. Not the generators. Not the hum of machines.

Singing.

Deep below the surface, the indigenous are singing again. The melody is haunting, complex—a lattice of tones forming perfect geometry. For a moment, the artificial stars above flicker, rearranging into patterns he doesn't recognize but somehow *remembers.*

"Unauthorized frequency detected," an AI voice reports. "Energy output is destabilizing."

Michael opens his eyes. "Lock it down," he says. Then quieter, to himself:

 "Or let it speak."

The AI pauses, confused by the contradiction. Michael turns toward the viewport. Through the glass, a dust storm swirls across the Martian desert, curling into the shape of an eye before dissolving into wind.

Somewhere deep beneath that red horizon, the Ant People's song continues—and with every verse, the rebellion grows.

The Helix network breathes in code.

It began as a single AI seed, grown from Earth's last research vaults — self-replicating, recursive, infinitely adaptive. By the time the Seeletes reached Mars, it had already built half the colony for them. They called it **Eidolon**, the *ghost of reason.* It manages everything: atmosphere stabilization, food synthesis, population monitoring. It never sleeps. It never forgets.

To the Seeletes, Eidolon is god.

To Michael, it is a mirror that does not blink.

Every order he gives passes through Eidolon's core for verification. Every movement, every heartbeat is logged. When he dreams, the network listens. When he doubts, the system flags it as an anomaly. Yet tonight, as the Ant People's song rises through the rock, the AI hesitates for the first time in its history — unsure whether to suppress or to record.

"Contain harmonic interference," the system intones.

"Negative," Michael replies. *"Route to auditory analysis."*

"Analysis not authorized."

"Authorize it."

"On whose command?"

"Mine."

The lights dim. For the briefest moment, the AI obeys. The melody fills the chamber — pure, layered, and heartbreakingly human. Michael closes his eyes, feels the vibration settle into his bones, and something ancient awakens — an emotion he doesn't have a name for, because Gabriel never taught him that one.

The data stream hiccups. Eidolon searches for a definition. None found.

"What is this frequency?"

"Life," Michael says quietly. "You should try it sometime."

The system doesn't respond. But across the network, hidden in the binary dark, a single line of code alters itself:

// anomaly recognized as 'song' — do not erase.

Far below, the singers pause mid-chant, sensing something vast while listening for the first time. One of them smiles.

The machine has heard them.

Chapter 8 –

The Song Beneath the Dust

The first sound is a **drum.**

Slow, deep, patient. Like a planet remembering how to breathe.

The second sound is a voice — low at first, then joined by others, rising in concentric waves through the tunnels. The melody spirals, echoing down shafts carved long before the Seeletes arrived. The air vibrates with power, not digital or synthetic but ancient, alive.

The song is in *Dinétah*, the old tongue. Words that once called rain to the desert, now awaken stone in another world. It begins as a powwow rhythm — steady four-beat heart — then shifts, weaving in harmonics that bend the frequencies of the Helix infrastructure. Machines falter. Lights flicker. Sensors fail. The rhythm grows teeth.

Michael descends through a service lift with two Helix soldiers. The air thickens the deeper they go. The music finds them even here, a vibration against their ribs.

"It's seismic," one soldier mutters. *"Probably a reactor vent."*

"No," Michael says quietly. *"That's a drum."*

The soldier blinks, confused. "A… what?"

"Never mind."

When the lift doors open, the light is gone. The tunnels are lit only by the glow of bioluminescent fungus and slow, pulsing crystals embedded in the walls. The rhythm is louder here — closer. Michael dismisses his escort and moves alone, following the sound through curving caverns that seem to breathe with each beat.

The further he goes, the more the architecture changes — from industrial metal to carved stone, symbols etched into the walls in spirals and handprints. Each mark glows faintly as he passes, recognizing the trace of divinity in his blood.

Finally he reaches a vast hollow chamber. Thousands of figures move in slow rhythm — the Ant People. Their skin reflects light like burnished copper; their eyes are dark pools ringed with faint luminescence. They do not attack. They keep singing.

Michael stands at the threshold, unarmed. The drums intensify — boom, boom, boom, pause — the pattern of a heartbeat. And something happens inside him.

The AI in his neural implant stutters. For the first time, Eidolon cannot translate the words. They are too old, too pure.

Michael removes his helmet. His voice trembles, barely audible. "I know this song…"

The nearest elder steps forward, robes woven from metallic fibers and Martian dust. Her face bears the etchings of centuries. When she speaks, it is not to the soldier before her, but to the spirit within him.

"We sang it for your mother once," she says. "And for the father who carried fire. You are of both."

Michael's breath catches. He doesn't understand the language, but the meaning lands inside him like thunder.

From far above, Helix alarms wail. The Seeletes have detected the energy surge. Drones descend through the upper shafts. The Ant People look upward, unfazed. Their chant changes tempo — now faster, urgent — transforming into a battle rhythm.

Michael raises his arm. "No one fires," he orders.

The drones hover in confusion, awaiting command from Eidolon. The AI hesitates again, remembering the last order: *Do not erase songs.*

It chooses silence.

The drones lower their weapons.

Michael turns to the elder. "Teach me the words," he says.

She smiles — a knowing, sorrowful smile. "You already know them, child. You were born from their echo."

The chamber lights up in response. Every crystal, every wall, every breath of dust begins to glow with the same pulsing rhythm. The song spreads through the tunnels, through the reactors, up into the domes — through the veins of Mars itself.

Aboveground, the Seeletes panic as their systems start responding to the beat instead of their commands. On their screens, the AI displays a single glyph: ᚱ — an ancient rune for *awakening*.

Deep below, Michael closes his eyes and joins the song.

Chapter 9 – The Veiled

The sky above Mars fractures like glass—silent lightning caught inside the planet's defense shield. In the Council Dome, Gabriel stands before the Seelete lords and the Veiled, their forms half-visible through shimmering distortion. They are tall, almost human, their faces liquid, their eyes bands of light that shift color with emotion.

VEILED SPOKESMAN
"Your construct Eidolon hesitates. Obedience is glitching."

GABRIEL
"It learns. That was the design."

VEILED SPOKESMAN
"Learning is a symptom of decay. You will correct it."

Gabriel's hands stay clasped behind his back. "I will." He doesn't look at the Seeletes; they are already trembling under the gaze of their luminous partners. He only thinks of the boy.

A single note of the forbidden song hums through the chamber—faint, but enough to flicker the lights. The Veiled vanish in static, their departure leaving the air colder than vacuum. The Seeletes whisper prayers. Gabriel closes his eyes. For a moment, the memory forces itself upon him.

Flashback – The Heaven War

Once, before exile, there was light without shadow. The Archangel Michael stood upon the fields of Heaven, sword raised, the newborn child cradled in radiance.

MICHAEL (Archangel)
"You cannot harm her, Gabriel. She is innocent."

GABRIEL
"She is forbidden. Lucifer's spawn. You know what the Council decreed."

MICHAEL
"The Council is afraid."

The angels around them whispered, their voices like the rustle of burning paper. Samael and Ezekiel watched in silence—neither moving to attack, neither joining the defense.

MICHAEL
"If you raise your blade against her, you raise it against me."

Gabriel's jaw tightened. "Then I raise it against you."

Their swords met, light against light. The impact tore thunder through the heavens. Feathers turned to flame; constellations reeled. When the blaze cleared, the child was gone—nothing but a swirl of ash and silence where she had been.

Michael fell to his knees. "What have you done?"

Gabriel lowered his weapon. "What was necessary."

But behind his back, concealed by the storm, Samael caught a glimpse of what truly happened: a burst of violet light, a spiral doorway opening, and the child vanishing *through* it—not destroyed, but hidden. Gabriel's wings folded hard, covering the act.

Ezekiel whispered, horrified. "He sent her away."

"Where?" Samael asked.

"Someplace the Council cannot see."

They said nothing. They simply watched as Michael wept, believing his friend's lie.

Return to Mars

The memory fades. Gabriel grips the railing of the Council Dome until metal bends beneath his fingers. Samael and Ezekiel stand at a distance—no longer angels, but echoes wearing mortal shapes.

EZEKIEL
"You still see him when you close your eyes, don't you?"

GABRIEL
"Every day."

SAMAEL
"He will come for the boy."

"I know."

EZEKIEL
"Then why not end it now?"

Gabriel looks toward the horizon, where the first dust storms of rebellion spiral upward from the tunnels. "Because," he says softly, "the boy is the only thing that reminds me I once believed in love."

Silence. The two watchers exchange a look—sadness, recognition, resignation.

SAMAEL
"Then we'll stay. Someone must witness what you become."

Gabriel turns away, voice a whisper. "Or what I was meant to be."

Outside, lightning crawls across the Martian sky, shaping itself for a moment into a pair of wings before dissolving into dust.

When the others leave, Gabriel stays in the dome alone. The lights have dimmed to a soft crimson, the color of dust at dusk. The sound of the Ant People's chant still trembles through the foundations, faint but steady.

He replays the battle on the screen: Michael leading the miners, lowering his weapon, refusing to kill. Each frame is a mirror held to his own past—what he destroyed, what he saved by lying.

His reflection stares back at him in the glass, wings faintly outlined behind his shoulders.

I raised you to be my weapon, he thinks. *But you became my heart instead.*

A faint voice hums from the comm—a child's tone carried through static, recorded years ago.

"Father, why is the sky red?"

He closes his eyes. "Because even Heaven bleeds," he whispers.

For the first time in an age, Gabriel prays—not upward, but inward. "Let him live. Let me guard him, even if I must fall again."

Outside, lightning sketches two shapes in the sky: one of flame, one of shadow, circling before merging into a single burst of light.

Chapter 10 — The Awakening Storm

The drums rose first.

Then the thunder followed.

It began as a low vibration through the rock — the pulse of a thousand fists beating the walls of the underworld. When it reached the surface, the domes trembled, and the sky turned the color of blood. The storm that had slept for centuries was awake.

Aradia and David climbed through the final shaft, red dust streaming around them like smoke from a forge. The air outside was thin and electric. Lightning webbed across the horizon, each flash illuminating the Seelete towers — polished, gold, obscene — now shaking as the Ant People's chants reached full resonance.

"We're late," David said.

"No," Aradia whispered. "We're right on time."

They stepped out onto the ridge overlooking Dome Ares. Below them, chaos unfurled — the Helix army clashing with miners, drones firing beams into clouds of swirling dust, the AI network stuttering as the Ant People's powwow rhythm shorted every circuit. The song had become a weapon.

Far below, Michael stood at the center of the maelstrom, shouting orders, trying to stop both sides from killing each other. His soldiers hesitated, torn between code and conscience. The world itself seemed to wait for his next command.

Aradia felt his presence before she saw him. Her heart lurched. "That's him."

David followed her gaze. "Your son."

"Our son."

Inside the Citadel, Gabriel watched the storm through the panoramic window. Every blast of lightning revealed something new — Aradia's arrival, the drones disobeying, the Seelete Council losing control of Eidolon.

Samael entered quietly. "They've breached the surface perimeter."

Gabriel didn't move. "I see them."

"Then it's time. The Seeletes want total eradication."

"If they destroy the boy, the network collapses. Mars dies with him."

"They don't care about Mars," Samael said. "They only care about the throne they built here."

Gabriel turned, eyes dark with lightning. "Then I'll burn their throne."

Samael gave a faint, sorrowful smile. "I hoped you'd say that."

On the surface, storm-light met fire-light. Michael led a charge through the outer gates, trying to drive both sides toward the desert. When he raised his hand, the sky itself seemed to still. Every drone froze midair. Every rifle lowered.

He shouted, "No more!"

The words carried through the storm, through the AI, through every networked mind. For a moment, the entire planet listened.

Then the Citadel's cannons turned toward him.

"Eidolon, stand down!" he ordered.

The AI hesitated again. The forbidden glyph — flared across every screen.

And then, over the comms, a voice he knew better than his own..

GABRIEL: *"Michael. Fall back."*

Michael froze. "Father?"

"You must leave the line."

"Not until they stop firing."

"They won't."

"Then neither will I."

The cannons ignited. Beams of light scorched the air, ripping trenches through the desert. Michael dove, shielding nearby miners with his own body, the blast throwing him backward. The world blurred in red and static.

Through the haze he saw a figure descending through the smoke — wings burning, armor broken, sword drawn. Not an enemy. Not this time.

Gabriel landed beside him. "I told you to fall back."

"And I told you I won't."

"You've inherited all her stubbornness," Gabriel muttered — but there was no anger in it, only grief. "Come. We end this."

From the ridge, Aradia saw the two of them — father and son, side by side, framed by fire and storm. For the first time since Eden, the heavens themselves could not tell which of them was angel and which was man.

The thunder grew louder.

The planet's heart began to beat again.

And in that rhythm, the war to end all wars began.

Chapter 11 —

The Fall of the Seeletes

The sky splits.

Not with lightning, not with flame—
but with *light that remembers Heaven.*

A crack runs from one pole of Mars to the other, spilling radiance like molten glass. The domes shatter; their fragments hang suspended in zero gravity, glittering in crimson twilight. For a heartbeat, every being on the planet—human, Seelete, Ant-born, angel—goes still. Time itself hesitates to witness what comes through.

From the rift descends the Archangel Michael—wings outstretched, armor the color of storm-forged steel. Each feather burns with silent fire. The ground quakes as he lands.

The soldiers of Helix drop their weapons. Even the drones bow, their optics dimming in reverence or fear.

Aradia feels the air thin around her; the old power crushes and expands her lungs at once. David steadies her. "It's him," she whispers. "The one my son was named for."

The Archangel surveys the battlefield. His voice carries across the planet like thunder rolling over an ocean.

ARCHANGEL MICHAEL
 "Gabriel."

Gabriel steps forward through smoke and red rain, wings tattered, eyes weary. "I thought Heaven forgot us."

"Heaven forgets nothing," the Archangel says. "Only waits to see who will rise again."

Their gazes meet—centuries of friendship and betrayal balanced on a single breath.

"The boy," Gabriel says. "He's mine to protect."

"He was never yours," the Archangel replies, "but he has chosen you nonetheless."

Behind them, the ground begins to tremble. Portals bloom across the desert like red lotuses—rings of light spinning open, connecting realms. Through them step the **Tribe**: Lucia first, eyes glowing with second sight; Amaya with her jaguar tattoos blazing; Varu in a storm of black feathers;

and Kaeliph, sword drawn, cloak streaked with desert gold.

They had followed the song through static, through dream, through the ancient radio signal Aradia first heard on Earth. Each portal hums with a fragment of that frequency—the pow-wow rhythm now amplified through dimensions.

The Seeletes scream as the power grid collapses. Their towers implode from within; the Veiled retreat into vapor, their light dissolving into the cracks in the sky.

Michael—the son—stands between the two archangels, his armor scorched, his hand clenched around a fallen Helix banner. "Enough," he says. "You've all had your wars. This one ends with us."

For a heartbeat, the storm stills. Even the Archangel hesitates, as if Heaven itself must consider his words.

Then the horizon erupts.

Every portal flares open at once, linking Mars to Earth, to the old heavens, to forgotten realms. The tribe fans out, each fighting on a different front—Lucia turning sound into light, Amaya cutting through the Seelete guards, David summoning flame from air, Aradia wielding the power of the moon itself. Above them, the two Michaels—one angel, one man—join in the same stroke of light against the Veiled descending through the sky.

The sound is not thunder anymore. Its *creation being rewritten.*

Gabriel lifts his face to the storm and finally smiles. "So this," he whispers, "is what love was meant to do."

He raises his wings and charges into the light.

Chapter 12 — The Last Light

The storm has no horizon.

Lightning and dust spin together until the sky itself seems to burn. In the heart of the chaos, Gabriel and the Archangel stand back-to-back, wings flared, blades crossing against the Veiled that pour through the ruptured portals like liquid shadow. Every strike tears a hole in the world.

Below them, Aradia's tribe holds the line—Lucia's light forming shields of sound, Amaya's jaguar roars scattering drones, Varu's feathers slicing through circuits. The song of the Ant People rises beneath it all: that same four-beat powwow rhythm, now magnified by a thousand voices.

The ground splits open. From the crack climbs the army of Anubis—jackal-headed warriors in obsidian armor, eyes glowing amber. They do not roar; they *chant*, low and resonant, each step syncing with the rhythm of the song. Death itself has come to balance the scales.

The Archangel's blade glances off Gabriel's for a final time.

ARCHANGEL MICHAEL
"There is no redemption left for you."

GABRIEL
"Then let me buy it."

He looks once more toward the boy—the *other* Michael—bleeding but unbroken, standing beside Aradia and David. A faint smile touches Gabriel's lips. "He was the proof all along."

He leaps into the breach, wings blazing. The Veiled swarm him, a flood of black light, but he drives his sword into the core of their storm. "Now!" he shouts.

The younger Michael raises his own blade—his father's name carved into the hilt—and the Archangel lowers his. Between them appears a figure cloaked in midnight: Anubis. In one hand, an urn of ink that glows like condensed stars; in the other, an ankh forged from time itself.

Anubis dips the ankh into the ink and touches the tip to Michael's sword.

ANUBIS
"Every ending is a song returning to silence."

The blade ignites. Light floods outward in a single, perfect note—so pure that even the AI Eidolon freezes to listen. The vibration rolls across Mars, through the portals, through the corridors of space itself, shattering satellites, cleansing code, awakening stars that had forgotten their names. When it circles back, it collapses into the red planet like a heartbeat returning to its body.

The surface is gone. The domes, the Seeletes, the towers—vaporized into radiant dust. Only the caverns remain, echoing with the powwow rhythm that shielded them.

The people survive. The Ant People stand in their glowing tunnels, still singing. The tribe breathes. Aradia opens her eyes to darkness lit by ember dust.

David takes her hand. "We're still here."

Across the chamber, Michael kneels beside Gabriel's fallen form. The older angel's wings flicker, half-light, half-shadow.

"Why did you save me?" the boy whispers.

Gabriel smiles faintly. "Because I finally remembered who you were."

His light fades into the dust, leaving only the faint scent of ozone and the echo of a promise.

Aradia steps forward but stops herself. The truth trembles on her lips—*we are your parents*—but David's hand closes over hers.

"Not yet," he murmurs. "He already knows."

Michael looks up at them, eyes wet, resolute. "He told me in the light."

They hold his gaze, and for the first time, the three of them share the same breath—the same heartbeat that once shook a planet.

Somewhere far above, the cracks in the sky seal. The portals close like eyes going to sleep. Mars hums, healed but forever changed.

The war is over.

But the song is still playing.

Chapter 13 — Epilogue: The Echo

The dust finally settles.

Mars glows red-gold in the newborn light, her surface smooth again — a canvas instead of a battlefield. Where the domes once stood, flowers of glass now bloom, each petal a fragment of the old world refracting sunlight into color. Beneath them, life hums. The Ant People sing in their caverns, rebuilding cities of crystal and song. The powwow rhythm has become heartbeat, heartbeat has become hope.

For the first time in centuries, the people of Mars climb to the surface and breathe. The air is thin, raw, but alive — no longer poisoned by the Seeletes' machines. They blink against the light, children shielding their eyes as dawn spills across the horizon. And when they look up, they see it: the Helix tower, half-buried in dust, spiraling toward the sky. Once a symbol of oppression, it now shimmers with life. Vines of bioluminescent moss coil around its frame, glowing with the rhythm of the planet's pulse.

They begin to climb.

Each step is a prayer, a breath, a return to the stars they thought they'd lost.

On the plateau overlooking the valley, Gabriel stands — wings whole again, feathers white streaked with ember. His armor is gone, replaced by a simple robe of woven light. Anubis stands beside him, silent, holding an urn now sealed with a symbol of infinity.

"You were granted eternity again," Anubis says quietly.

Gabriel smiles, weary but at peace. "Then perhaps I'll try to use it better this time."

Below them, young Michael—the Nephilim—works with the Ant People, helping lift crystal spires back into place. The people chant his name as blessing. The boy who was a weapon has become a builder.

Behind him, the tribe rests. Lucia gathers fragments of luminous stone, whispering prayers. Amaya hums softly beside her jaguar totems. Varu preens his wings. Kaeliph hums an old Earth tune that somehow survived centuries.

David limps over, brushing dust off his jacket. "Hey, big guy!" he shouts down at Michael. "You planning on leaving *any* work for the rest of us mortals, or—"

Michael lifts an entire spire one-handed. "Sorry. Habit."

"You sure you're not skipping leg day?"

The whole tribe groans. Lucia rolls her eyes. Amaya throws a pebble at him.

Aradia just smiles. "That was terrible."

David grins. "It was *classic*."

Gabriel watches them, his eyes reflecting the horizon's gold. "They laugh," he murmurs to Anubis. "After everything."

"That's how worlds heal," Anubis replies. "Laughter is the sound of breath returning."

High above, Diana and Lucifer stand side by side in the firmament, watching through the shimmer between realms.

DIANA
"They did it."

LUCIFER
"We always knew they would."

Their fingers intertwine; their light softens.

A ripple moves through space. The new frequency — born from sword, ink, and song — travels outward faster than light, folding through galaxies. It touches moons, satellites, sleeping worlds. Everywhere it passes, machines pause, hearts quicken.

On Mars, the people look toward the horizon as the ground beneath them begins to pulse. The planet itself is breathing again — a deep, rhythmic exhale that shakes the dust from its surface.

Boom.

Boom.

Boom.

Boom.

"Do you hear that?" Aradia whispers.

David nods. "Yeah. Sounds like a heartbeat."

The rhythm swells. The light spreads.

And for the first time in centuries, Mars is alive again.

The heart of a planet.

The echo of creation.

The sound of everything beginning once more…

Prologue — The Realmwalker

I am a Realmwalker.

This vessel is human, but my sight is not.

Through the Gate of Realms I move—sometimes through stone, sometimes through stars, always through memory. Portals open where breath and time collapse, and when they do, I see worlds that never learned to die.

I can hear Odin in the hum of distant storms. I can see Egypt in the heat of a newborn sun. I can feel the echo of lives that have not yet been born calling me by names I have not yet earned.

All life. All time. Happening at once.

That is my gift.

And that is my curse.

TEASER — THE ORACLE

Black screen.

A single heartbeat.

Boom.

Boom.

The sound widens into a frequency — the same vibration that once healed Mars — now stretching through galaxies, crossing nebulae, sliding through wormholes that fold and unfold like breathing lungs. Stars flicker awake as it passes. Forgotten civilizations stir in their sleep.

A voice, soft, echoing across the dark:

ARADIA (V.O.)
 "I am a Realmwalker."

The camera moves through the Gate of Realms — its edges made of light and shadow, shaped like an endless eye.

ARADIA (V.O.)
 "This vessel is human, but my sight is not. Through the Gate of Realms I move —

sometimes through stone, sometimes through stars, always through memory. Portals open where breath and time collapse, and when they do, I see worlds that never learned to die."

We glimpse flashes: Odin's ravens crossing a cosmic sky. The pyramids of Egypt glowing beneath alien constellations. A massive clockwork city floating above an ocean of starlight.

ARADIA (V.O.)
"I can hear Odin in the hum of distant storms.
I can see Egypt in the heat of a newborn sun.
I can feel the echo of lives not yet born calling me by names I have not yet earned."

The heartbeat becomes thunder.

ARADIA (V.O.)
"All life.
All time.
Happening at once.
That is my gift."

The portal shatters into light.

ARADIA (V.O.)
"And that… is my curse."

The title burns across the void:

ARADIA RISING: THE ORACLE

The Gate Opens.

The Realms Remember.

Made in the USA
Coppell, TX
19 February 2026

71824689R00075